A Cake for Dinner

WITHDRAWN

by Sue Graves

Illustrated by Richard Watson

Crabtree Publishing Company

www.crabtreebooks.com

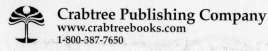

Crabtree Publishing Company
www.crabtreebooks.com
1-800-387-7650

616 Welland Ave.
St. Catharines, ON
L2M 5V6

PMB 59051, 350 Fifth Ave.
59th Floor,
New York, NY

Published by Crabtree Publishing in 2011

Series Editor: Jackie Hamley
Editor: Reagan Miller
Series Advisors: Dr. Hilary Minns, Catherine Glavina
Series Designer: Peter Scoulding
Project Coordinator: Kathy Middleton

Text © Sue Graves 2010
Illustration © Richard Watson 2010

Printed in Canada/102017/MQ20170731

First published in 2010
by Franklin Watts
(A division of Hachette
Children's Books)

The rights of the author and the
illustrator of this Work have
been asserted.

**Library and Archives Canada
Cataloguing in Publication**

Graves, Sue
  A cake for dinner / by Sue Graves ; illustrated by
Richard Watson.

(Tadpoles)
ISBN 978-0-7787-0572-7 (bound).--
ISBN 978-0-7787-0583-3 (pbk.)

  I. Watson, Richard, 1980- II. Title. III. Series:
Tadpoles (St. Catharines, Ont.)

PZ7.G8525Ca 2011   j823'.92   C2011-900147-0

**Library of Congress
Cataloging-in-Publication Data**

Graves, Sue, 1950-
  A cake for dinner / by Sue Graves ; illustrated by
Richard Watson.
    p. cm. -- (Tadpoles)
  Summary: Molly and her mother make a mess while
trying to bake a cake for Grandma's visit.
  ISBN 978-0-7787-0583-3 (pbk. : alk. paper) --
  ISBN 978-0-7787-0572-7 (reinforced library binding :
alk. paper)
  [1. Cake--Fiction. 2. Baking--Fiction. 3. Mothers and
daughters--Fiction. 4. Picture puzzles.] I. Watson,
Richard, ill. II. Title. III. Series.

PZ7.G7754Cak 2011
[E]--dc22
                                        2010052353

Here is a list of the words in this story.
Common words:

a	is	oh	was
and	made	said	you
but	make	then	
came	Mom	this	
for	no	to	

Other words:

cake	Grandma	yes
coming	let's	yum
dear	mess	
dinner	Molly	

Grandma was coming to dinner.

"Let's make a cake,"
said Mom.

But Molly made
a mess.

Mom made
a mess, too.

Then Molly and Mom made a mess!

"Oh dear," said Mom.
"No cake for dinner!"

Grandma came.

"This is for you,"
Grandma said.

"A cake for dinner!" said Molly. "Yes!"

"Yum!"

Puzzle Time

a

b

Can you find these pictures in the story?

c

d

Which pages are
the pictures from?

Turn over for the answers!

Answers

The pictures come from these pages:
a. pages 8 and 9
b. pages 4 and 5
c. pages 20 and 21
d. pages 12 and 13

Notes for adults

Tadpoles are structured to provide support for early readers. The stories may also be used by adults for sharing with young children.

Starting to read alone can be daunting. **Tadpoles** help by listing the words in the book for a preview before reading. **Tadpoles** also provide strong visual support and repeat words and phrases. These books will both develop confidence and encourage reading and rereading for pleasure.

If you are reading this book with a child, here are a few suggestions:

1. Make reading fun! Choose a time to read when you and the child are relaxed and have time to share the story.

2. Look at the picture on the front cover and read the blurb on the back cover. What might the story be about? Why might the child like it?

3. Look at the list of words on page two. Can the child identify most of the words?

4. Encourage the child to retell the story using the jumbled picture puzzle on pages 22-23.

5. Discuss the story and see if the child can relate it to his or her own experiences, or perhaps compare it to another story he or she knows.

6. Give praise! Children learn best in a positive environment.

If you enjoyed this book, why not try another **TADPOLES** story?
Please see the back cover for more **TADPOLES** titles.
Visit **www.crabtreebooks.com** for other **Crabtree** books.